Eggs with Legs

Eggs
with Legs

JUDY DELTON

Illustrated by Alan Tiegreen

A YEARLING BOOK

Published by
Bantam Doubleday Dell Books for Young Readers
a division of
Bantam Doubleday Dell Publishing Group, Inc.
1540 Broadway
New York, New York 10036

ISBN: 0-440-40979-9

Printed in the United States of America

May 1996

10 9 8 7 6 5 4 3 2 1

CWO

For Beverly Vavoulis
Lexiphanic, orthodontic, lethonomic,
Sesquipedalic, yardarmic, defenestratic:
Words are our bond, our life and our end.
Thank you, dear Beverly, for being my friend.

Contents

nursing home, Molly wondered how
Roger would like to be called a geezer. Or
a pip-squeak.

"...d her know we're there," said Mrs. P...

CHAPTER 1
The Fake Holiday

"**D**o you know what day it is next week?" asked Molly Duff.

"Sure, I know," said Sonny Stone. "It's Sunday. That's a day next week!"

"And Monday and Tuesday and Wednesday!" said Tracy Barnes, laughing.

"And Thursday and Friday and Saturday!" said Tim Noon. "Those are all days that come next week!"

The Pee Wees were on their way to their meeting at Mrs. Peters's house. She was their leader. They were early, so they sat on a park bench in the sun because spring felt so good. The snow was gone and they were all eager for summer, when they could ride bikes and go to the beach and eat Popsicles.

"That's not what I mean," said Molly. "There's a holiday next week."

"What holiday?" asked Rachel Myers. "There's no holiday. Christmas is over and it's not the Fourth of July yet."

"You mean Easter, I'll bet," said Kevin Moe.

Molly liked Kevin. He and Jody George were her two favorites of the boys in Troop 23. Jody was handicapped and had a wheelchair Molly loved to ride in. She even wished she had one of her own.

Jody was away on a spring trip with his parents in Florida. His family did a lot of traveling. But Kevin was here, and Molly

was almost ready to say Easter *was* the holiday she meant. But she couldn't lie. Even though no one would know.

She shook her head and said, "No, it's April Fools' Day."

Roger White groaned. "That's no holiday!" he said. "Where do you see ads that say 'Celebrate April Fools' with us,' or 'Give your mom a tulip plant for April Fools' Day'?"

The Pee Wees all seemed to agree with Roger.

"We don't get the day off from school," said Rachel.

"And they don't even make cards that say 'Happy April Fools' Day,' " said Patty Baker. "I never saw them, anyway. It must be kind of like a fake holiday."

"If it were a real holiday," said Lisa Ronning, "Mrs. Peters would have a Pee Wee party for us. And what would she put on a cake? What does an April Fool look like?"

Kenny Baker nodded. "On the Fourth of July you can have red-white-and-blue frosting. And on Christmas you have red and green, and on Easter you have candy eggs and rabbits. But there's nothing you can put on an April Fools' cake. No way. April Fools' is not a holiday."

The Pee Wees looked bored and disgusted with Molly's idea. They began to talk about other things, like the ice rink that had melted and the crabby new teacher in second grade.

"I think April Fools' *is* a holiday," said Molly's best friend, Mary Beth Kelly.

It felt good to Molly to have at least one person who agreed with her. But maybe Mary Beth was just being loyal. Maybe she felt sorry for Molly. Maybe she really believed it was a silly idea but didn't want to hurt her best friend's feelings. Molly *hated* pity.

"I mean, it's on the calendar, you know. My calendar says 'April Fools' Day,' as big as life. If that's not proof, I don't know what is."

But Molly did not need proof. She *knew* she was right.

"It doesn't matter if the others don't celebrate," Mary Beth added. "You and I can. What should we do?"

"Well, the way people celebrate is to play tricks on each other," said Molly. "I think we should think of a good one to play on Roger."

Roger White was the meanest Pee Wee in Troop 23. He was always tripping people or hitting them, or showing off. On a recent farm visit, he had pushed Tracy into the muddy pigpen.

6

The girls looked at him. He was dangling a rubber spider down the neck of Sonny's T-shirt. Sonny was screaming.

"He deserves a good trick," said Mary Beth. "Let's think of something spectacular!"

"He'll do something mean to get back at us, though," said Molly.

"Not if he doesn't know who did it," said Mary Beth. "Where can we find some tricks to play? Do you think there's a book of April Fools' tricks?"

"I think we can make up our own," said Molly mysteriously.

She got up and started down the street to Mrs. Peters's house, and Mary Beth and the others followed. When they got there, they went down Mrs. Peters's steps and into her basement. On top of the big table where they had their meetings was a

big pink plastic rabbit. It was inflatable, and it had an orange carrot in its plastic paw.

"Well!" said their leader. "It's a shame to be indoors on such a nice day. If the backyard wasn't so muddy, we could have our meeting outside. But we'll just open up the windows and let some of the spring come in."

After she did this, she counted to be sure all eleven Pee Wees were present, and then she said, "There are two holidays coming up soon, and I thought we would talk about them and see if we can do something special to celebrate."

"See," whispered Mary Beth. "Mrs. Peters is going to tell us how to celebrate April Fools' day!"

Everyone there wondered if Molly was right—maybe this *was* one of the holidays Mrs. Peters had in mind.

CHAPTER 2
The Big Plan

"The first holiday that is coming up," Mrs. Peters said, "is Easter. And I thought we might dye eggs and make baskets for shut-ins.

"The other one is Mother's Day. And of course we want to do something nice for our mothers."

Mrs. Peters had let Molly down! All the Pee Wees looked at Molly, as if to say "See, I told you so! April Fools' Day isn't a holiday!"

"Hey, Roger can't celebrate Mother's Day!" shouted Sonny. "He doesn't have a mother. You have to have a mother to celebrate."

Roger looked angry. He didn't like to be told he was missing anything, especially anything as important as a mother. Molly felt a little sorry for him. A trick was one thing, but to hurt his feelings was another.

"Tim doesn't have a dad either," Roger shouted to Sonny. "What is *he* going to do on Father's Day?"

Mrs. Peters held up her arms in alarm. "Often," she said, "people have others who take the role of a parent. Like an aunt, or a friend, or an uncle. It doesn't have to be an actual parent."

"Mrs. Peters has opened up a can of worms now," whispered Rachel to Molly. "This is one of those social issues people

11

don't want to face. My mom told me so," she added wisely. "My mom's going to school to get a degree in psychology. She's going to be a psychologist."

Rachel's dad was a dentist. Sometimes Rachel liked to show off and brag about her family, but she could also be a very good friend. When Molly had shared her pen pal with Rachel, she had been very grateful. And when Molly's dad had lost his job, Rachel's mother had sent a nice dinner over to the Duffs to cheer them up.

"Now that her mom's in school, she thinks she knows everything," whispered Mary Beth to Molly.

"Well, she's right, you know," said Molly. "Mrs. Peters did open up a can of worms."

Roger's eyes were red now, and so were Tim's. What would their leader do? Maybe Rachel would have to phone her mother and have her come to the meeting and bring her textbooks and help out!

"It wasn't Mrs. Peters's fault," said Mary Beth. "It was Sonny's. He had to go and yell at Roger about not having a mother."

Mrs. Peters took the "can of worms" into the laundry room. She put her arms around Roger and Tim and talked to them privately. When they came back they were smiling. At least a little.

Mrs. Peters went on with the meeting as if there had been no can of worms.

"I think it's time we start planning what we will do for these two holidays, Pee Wee–wise," she said. "Besides celebrating, we want to do something to help others, and to earn a holiday badge. I thought we could combine the two days and get one badge, called a spring badge."

The Pee Wees cheered. They loved

badges, and badge talk, and earning badges. They loved to collect them and pin them on their blouses and shirts.

Molly got out her notebook, because she felt better writing everything down. She loved to make lists. And keep track of what to do for badges.

"I thought we could do three things to earn this badge," said their leader.

Molly wrote a big "1" in her notebook.

"Number one is, I thought of dyeing eggs and making up colorful Easter baskets for the people in the nursing home. You can all be thinking of what else you'd like to put in your baskets."

Molly wrote down, "Find things to put in baskets."

"I think they would enjoy that," Mrs. Peters continued, "and we could combine it with a visit. Many of the senior citizens there don't have visitors, and we could brighten their day by talking to them, and listening to them."

"Some of them can't hear," said Roger. "I know one old geezer there who doesn't know what you're saying. And their stories are boring."

The Pee Wees glared at Roger. They did not like to hear him call old people geezers. Some of them had grandparents in the nursing home. Molly wondered how Roger would like to be called a geezer. Or a pip-squeak.

"They know we're there," said Mrs. Peters, glaring at Roger. "Whether they can hear us or not."

Hands were waving. "Mrs. Peters," called Ashley Baker. Ashley was Patty and Kenny Baker's cousin from California. She was a temporary Scout because she was just visiting. But she was in Minnesota so much that she didn't seem like a temporary Pee Wee to Molly.

"In California we went to the Golden West Retirement home and cooked dinner for senior citizens on St. Patrick's Day. We made everything green. Green beans, green peas, green chicken, green potatoes, even green cake."

The Pee Wees stared at Ashley. They had never heard of green potatoes. They do strange things in California, thought Molly. Ashley always told stories about things that no one ever did in Minnesota. Maybe it was because of the earthquakes. Maybe pictures fell off the walls and onto peoples' heads and made them odd.

"That's very nice," said Mrs. Peters. "I am sure the seniors enjoyed the dinner very much."

"They did," said Ashley. "They all had seconds."

"But I think a basket will be enough for us to handle."

"Basket, handle, get it? Handle!" cried Tracy, who loved riddles and crossword puzzles.

"The next holiday is Mother's Day, and as our second thing to do to earn our badges I thought it would be nice to think of something we could do that would be extraspecial for our mothers," said Mrs. Peters. "Or our aunts or grandmas or whomever you wish to honor on Mother's Day," she added quickly.

Hands were waving again.

"I want to honor my dad on Mother's Day," said Roger.

"He can't do that, can he, Mrs. Peters?" asked Sonny. "Maybe an aunt, but you can't make a dad into a mother!"

Mrs. Peters is treading on thin ice, thought Molly, remembering something her grandma always said. Mrs. Peters has hurt Roger's feelings once today; she has to watch out.

"Yes," their leader said firmly. "If Roger wants to honor his dad on Mother's Day, it is fine."

"Ho ho, are you going to give him a bottle of perfume, or a bunch of flowers?" taunted Sonny.

"Men like flowers as well as women," said Ashley. "And I give my dad after-shave lotion, and that's just like perfume. Sonny is a sexist!"

All the girls booed Sonny. Mrs. Peters frowned and held up her hands for quiet.

"Flowers and perfume are for people. Men *or* women. Now let's talk about what else we can think of for Mother's Day. Maybe *doing* something nice would be better than giving things."

"Breakfast in bed," suggested Tracy.

"Cleaning the house," said Kevin.

"Carrying groceries in," said Mary Beth. "I do that a lot."

"Those are all good suggestions," said their leader. "But let's try to think of something out of the ordinary. Something you've never done for them before. We have a week to think about it, and by our next meeting you can tell us what you've decided. And now for the third project. In spring things look dirty, and I thought it would be nice to help clean up the park, and maybe rake yards for some people who can't do it themselves. Sort of a community service springtime cleanup."

Molly wrote everything down.

"Boy, that's a lot of work for one badge!" said Lisa.

"She's right," said Mary Beth. "This spring badge is too much work."

Mrs. Peters looked as if *she* had done a

lot of work. Just at this meeting! She looks worn out just from trying to keep the Pee Wees from insulting each other and arguing, thought Molly.

After the good deeds were reported, and the songs sung, and the cupcakes eaten, the meeting was over.

On the way out Ashley said, "I think Mrs. Peters should have included St. Patrick's Day. After all, that's a spring holiday too."

"Well then, so is Valentine's Day," said Rachel. "And St. Patrick's is only for the Irish."

Ashley stamped her foot. "It is *not*," she said.

"Well, I think April Fools' is just as important as that," said Mary Beth.

Rat's knees, thought Molly. Mrs. Peters had decided on the two holidays. There was no use arguing about it. Easter and

Mother's Day were badge makers. All the others would have to be celebrated behind their leader's back! And April Fools' was Molly's choice for that!

CHAPTER 3

Up to No Good

When Molly got home she added more things to her notebook. She made a list of what she would have to come up with to get this badge.

First she would have to think of something unusual to put in her basket with the dyed eggs, to take to the nursing home. She wrote down a few ideas with a question mark after each one. Jelly beans? No, that was not unusual. A comb? Maybe. A pencil? They probably had pencils in the nursing home. She left some blank pages in case she thought of something better.

On the next page she wrote some treats for her mother. Candy? Too common. Flowers? The same. She could pick flowers in the garden, no sense in *paying* for them. What could she do that she'd never done, and that would really be a surprise? She left a blank page there too, and put a giant question mark. This wasn't going too well.

The third thing she did not need to plan. Cleanup day was cleanup day. Someone would give her a rake or a rag and tell her where to go and what to do. No, it was the first two she had to worry about.

But April Fools' came before Easter, and before Mother's Day. So if she wanted to play a trick on Roger it would have to be the first thing she thought about.

On the next page of the notebook she wrote, "Think of good April Fools' tricks to play on people. (Especially Roger.) Do it soon."

The next day after school, Molly caught up with Mary Beth.

"We have to work on our April Fools' trick right away," she said. "I have an idea."

The girls went over to Mary Beth's house and sat on her porch.

"Tell me," said Mary Beth. "What's your idea?"

"Well, I think our trick should be on Roger," said Molly. "I mean he's the one who is always playing tricks on other people. I think we should get back at him."

"April Fools' is a perfect time to do it," agreed Mary Beth. "It should be a real

good trick, though, like a pail of water falling on his head or ice cubes going down his back."

Molly shook her head. "I've got a better idea," she said. "What does Roger hate the most?"

Mary Beth thought. "He hates to be teased about girls," she said.

"Exactly!" said Molly. "I think we should pretend to be a girl who likes him a lot. We can write him real mushy notes and he'll hate it!"

"Will we sign our names?" asked her friend.

"Of course not!" said Molly in alarm. "We'll put 'from an admirer.' "

"Then he'll think some girl is after him," said Mary Beth, "and he'll hate it!"

Molly nodded. "And the best part is, it

isn't *real* mean or nasty, it's just a little bit nasty. I mean my mom and dad wouldn't like us to do something really bad."

"I don't think we should tell them, though," said Mary Beth.

"Of course not!" said Molly.

Mary Beth ran to get her perfumed notes and envelopes, the ones with the flowers on them.

"I'll do the writing," said Molly. "I think we should write at least three mushy notes and put them in his mailbox one at a time."

"We could put one in his desk," said Mary Beth.

"Good idea," said Molly. She wrote, "Dear Roger," and then she frowned. "I don't know how to write mushy stuff," she said.

"Let's go down to the drugstore and

look at the greeting cards," said Mary Beth. "We can copy those."

The girls dashed downtown. There were racks and racks of cards in the store. They went to the ones that said "Husbands, Wives, Loved Ones." One by one they read them.

"Here's a good one!" said Molly. "Listen. 'I dream of you all night and day. Come be my love and make my day. Happy birthday.' "

"Let's leave off the 'happy birthday' part," said Mary Beth sensibly.

Molly copied the rest of it. "We need two more," she said.

"Here is an anniversary greeting 'to my wife,' " said Mary Beth. "We can just use the verse. 'You've been by my side, through joy and tears. Let's love each other for many more years.' "

"Have we been by his side?" asked Molly, frowning.

Mary Beth stamped her foot. "This is a trick," she said. "It's not a lie-detector test!"

"Okay," said Molly. "Now number three."

" 'For one I love from afar,' " read Mary Beth. " 'A secret pal.' " She picked it up.

" 'I've loved you in secret, my heart has been true. Call me your kitten, if you love me too. Your secret pal.' I think this is the best one. We should send it last."

"But he can't call us his kitten, he won't know who it is," said Molly.

"That doesn't matter!" said Mary Beth. "That's the joke! He keeps getting these love notes but he'll never know who sent them! That's a great April Fools' trick."

"Is it too mean?" asked Molly.

Mary Beth shook her head. "It won't *hurt* him," she said. "He can just throw them away and not show them to anyone. But it will make him mad, nonetheless."

"Okay," said Molly, copying all three cards. Just as she was finishing, a clerk came over and said, "You're supposed to buy the cards, not copy them."

"We're just leaving," said Mary Beth sweetly.

Mary Beth seems better at planning tricks than I am, thought Molly.

When they got back to Mary Beth's, Molly copied the three verses on three different pieces of Mary Beth's flowered smelly stationery. They put each into an envelope and wrote "Roger White" on the front.

"Thursday is April Fools'," Molly said. "Let's deliver them the night before."

On Wednesday after school, the girls

went to Roger's house. When no one was around, Molly snuck up to the mailbox and slipped the first envelope into the box. Then the girls ran home.

At school the next day they waited until recess. Then Mary Beth handed Molly the second envelope. She slipped it into Roger's desk on top of his binder. Then they went out to play.

After recess they kept their eyes on Roger. They saw him take his binder out. Then he saw the card. It dropped to the floor and he picked it up. He opened it and sniffed it and turned red. Then he put it back in his desk.

"This is a great trick!" said Mary Beth, laughing, on the way home. "He has no idea who it is who loves him!"

"I wonder if he got the first one," said Molly.

"Of course he did," said Mary Beth.

"Everyone gets their mail. It's a law. You've got to read it."

"Where should we put the last one?" asked Molly. "The one that says he should call his secret pal 'kitten'!"

"Somewhere where we can see him open it," said Mary Beth. The girls thought.

"How about in his bike saddlebag?" said Molly. "Or his backpack."

"His bike," said Mary Beth. The girls ran to the bike rack. Roger's bike was there! Its license plate said "Roger." They popped the note into the saddlebag.

Then they hid behind a tree till Roger came. He opened the bag to put his books in and saw the card. He didn't open it. He just rode off toward home.

"Rat's knees!" said Molly. "He could have opened it so we could watch."

On the way home Molly felt let down.

Their trick was over too soon and not very exciting.

But when she got home she found out that the excitement was just beginning. Her mother had the phone in her hand.

"It's for you, Molly," she said. "I believe it's Roger White."

CHAPTER 4

"Hi, Kitten"

Molly stared at the phone in her mother's hand. *Roger?* Why in the world would Roger call her at home? He never called her! Her stomach flip-flopped. His call had something to do with the April Fools' trick. The trick had gone wrong! Molly took the phone and said, "Hello?"

"Hi, kitten," said Roger.

"What did you say?" asked Molly. She must have heard him wrong!

"Kitten. You said in your letter to call you 'kitten.' "

Molly's stomach did another flip-flop. She had just told herself that the trick was boring. Well, it did not feel boring any longer! How did Roger know she had sent the letters? Could he read her mind? Had he traced her fingerprints on the notes?

What could she say to him? If she denied she wrote the letters, it would be what her father called a bald-faced lie. She couldn't keep lying.

And if she said yes, that she wrote them, then she would have to claim she loved Roger! Was wild about him! That was a lie too! Of course she didn't love him. She was too young to really have boyfriends. And when she was old enough, her boyfriend would be Jody, or Kevin. Never ever Roger! He was no one she would choose for a friend, let alone a boyfriend.

Molly didn't know what to do, so she

hung up the phone. She called Mary Beth and told her the awful news.

"How could he know it was you?" Mary Beth asked.

Molly noticed that Mary Beth did not say *"us."* She said *"you"*!

"I don't know!" cried Molly. "I just know I'm in trouble!"

"Well, Roger doesn't want a girlfriend, you can be sure of that," said Mary Beth.

But the next day at school it appeared that he did! And he wanted Molly!

"Hey, you guys," he said to everyone on the playground, "look at the love letters I got from Molly Duff! She wants to be my girlfriend. She wants me to call her 'kitten.' "

Everyone was reading the April Fools' letters and laughing at her! Molly turned bright red and ran into the school. But that didn't help. As the children came in, they

all turned around and pointed at her. Molly would have to quit school and move away. That was all there was to it. She'd have to get out of town and start a new life.

On the way home Roger followed her and Mary Beth and kept saying, "Hey, kitten, we have years together ahead of us!" Then he made a terrible kissing noise with his mouth that made Molly cringe. Molly made a resolution that she would never never never play another April Fools' joke in her whole life. It was definitely not her favorite holiday anymore. Probably Mrs. Peters and the others were right—it had never been a holiday to begin with!

Back at Molly's the girls tried to think of what to do.

"This is an emergency," said Mary Beth.

While they were thinking, the phone

rang. Molly's parents were not home, so Mary Beth answered it. She signaled to Molly that it was Roger. "How did you know it was Molly?" Mary Beth asked. Molly thought she could at least have said "*us*"!

Mary Beth listened. Then she hung up. "He saw you from his bedroom window when you put the card in his mailbox. And he saw you near his bike. He said he'd have known anyway, because you're the only one who makes little circles when you dot your *i*'s. He says he wants to go to a movie with you Saturday."

Now Molly burst into tears. "I thought you said Roger didn't want a girlfriend!" she cried. "This was supposed to be a trick on Roger, not a trick on *me*!"

"It backfired," said Mary Beth. "How could I know that?"

After a little while Mary Beth said, "There's only one thing to do, I guess."

"Move to China or somewhere," said Molly.

Mary Beth thought about that. She shook her head. "Your dad and mom would have to get jobs there," she said. "You can't move alone. No, I think you'll have to go out with him. He'll get tired of it and then you can have a fight and break up and forget all about it."

Molly stared at Mary Beth. "Are you kidding?" she said. "I am not going to be Roger's girlfriend!" It was fine for Mary Beth to suggest this awful thing. *She* didn't have to do it! Even though the trick was both of theirs!

"Well, what else can you do?" Mary Beth said.

Molly sighed. "There's always the

truth," she said. "I'll have to tell him it was a joke. An April Fool."

"He'll really be mad then," said Mary Beth. "He doesn't like to be the butt of a joke."

"Well, he's always doing it to other people," said Molly.

"But he's not a good loser," said Mary Beth. "He plays jokes, but he doesn't let anyone play jokes on *him*."

"I'll write him another letter," said Molly, "and tell him it was an April Fool."

After Mary Beth left, that was what Molly did. She wrote that she was sorry and then she took the note (on nonsmelly paper) and put it in Roger's mailbox. When she got home, the phone was ringing.

"Why is Roger calling so often?" asked her dad.

"He likes me," Molly said, sighing. She took the phone from her dad.

On the other end Roger said, "Hey, that was no trick. You really like me, I know you do. And Saturday we've got a date. I'm coming over to take you to a movie at two o'clock. Then my dad wants you to come over for dinner. You know, like one of the family."

Things were not getting better! Molly had heard about things like this on the TV talk shows! She would hide on Saturday! She would run away!

All week Molly couldn't think of anything except the "date"! As it got closer and closer she knew she couldn't hide. Her parents would come looking for her when Roger arrived, and they would be very worried if they couldn't find her. And if she ran away, they would be even more worried! It looked as if she had to face the music. Bite the bullet.

It took all her courage to tell her parents she was going to a movie with Roger and over to his house afterward.

Her father frowned and her mother smiled. "Well, I think it's nice to get along with all your classmates, dear," her mother said. "After all, Roger is a Pee Wee too."

But when Roger came to the door at two o'clock, he wasn't alone. Sonny was with him, and so was Tim. When she opened the door, all three of them shouted, "April Fool!" and began to laugh.

"I really had you fooled, didn't I?" roared Roger. "You really thought I'd go to a movie with you! And ask you over for supper! Hey, that would be the day! That will teach you to play a joke on Roger

White," he said. "The April Fool is on you!"

Sonny and Tim were bent over laughing with Roger now. Molly thought of acting hurt. But this trick had gone far enough. The buck stopped here, as she'd heard her dad say.

"That was a good joke on me," she told Roger.

"You bet it was," he roared. "It wasn't a joke on *me*, it was on *you*," he repeated. "Say it, tell me you were the Fool."

Molly sighed. This was awful. "It was your joke," said Molly. "I was the Fool."

The boys ran down the street, whooping and hollering, and Molly went into the house. She'd never live this down. Roger wouldn't let anyone forget it. It was the very last April Fools' Day she would celebrate in her life.

But even though she felt humiliated, she

was relieved. She didn't have to go to a movie with Roger! He didn't want her to be his girlfriend! Whew. It had been a close call. But she was free.

CHAPTER **5**

The Great Idea

To put the joke that had backfired out of her mind entirely, Molly got out her notebook and tore out the April Fools' pages. She ripped them into small pieces and threw them in the wastebasket. Now she would concentrate on the Easter baskets and Mother's Day.

At the next Pee Wee meeting, everyone talked about what he or she was going to do for his or her mother that was new and different. Almost all of them had ideas.

"Mrs. Peters!" shouted Rachel. "We're taking my mom out for dinner because she's so tired from all the work she does going to graduate school. My dad and I made reservations at this place called The Trout Farm where they give you a pole and you catch your own fish and then a cook fries it for your dinner right by the lake. I'll bet no one else thought of that!"

"Hey, that's not fishing," said Roger. "They've got this little pond there and they put the fish right under your nose to catch. You could reach in and grab one with your hand! They may as well hand you a fish when you come in the door. That's no sport, my dad told me so."

"It does sound mean," said Lisa. "Those poor little fishies don't even have a chance to hide!"

"The animal cruelty people wouldn't

like it if they knew," said Kenny. "Some-one could report them."

Rachel's Mother's Day plan was not getting a lot of positive response. Instead of everyone congratulating her on her clever idea, they were booing her.

"Well, I think my mom will like it!" said Rachel. She sat down so hard, her curls bounced.

"She'll only like it if she's an animal hater," said Tim.

"My mom does not hate animals," said Rachel. She looked as if she might cry. "Anyway, fish are food," she added. "That's what they're for. To eat."

"I've got one in a bowl," said Patty Baker. "His name is Spot. I wouldn't want to eat him!"

Now the rest of the Pee Wees told about their aquariums and their guppies and how pretty they were.

"I went to Sea World in Florida," said Tracy. "And they have these nice big dolphins that smile at you and do tricks. I'd never want to eat one of *those*."

Rachel was outnumbered. Molly went over to her and said, "I like to fish. And I like to eat the sunfish my mom fries at the lake."

"So do I!" said Ashley. "I go salmon fishing with my dad, and lots of times we have lobster right on the beach at home."

Mrs. Peters held her hand up for silence. At least two people defended Rachel, thought Molly. Rachel seemed grateful.

"Now let's hear some other fresh Mother's Day ideas," said their leader.

"I'm cooking my dad a big thick steak," said Roger.

"And some poor cow died for that,"

said Ashley. "I mean, a cow has more feelings than a fish."

Molly wished they would get off the subject of food.

It looked as if Mrs. Peters did too. "No more food talk," she said.

Lots of the Pee Wees told about foodless plans. They announced that they would run errands and spade gardens and sort laundry and push the grocery cart at the market. Others were going to paint pictures or scrub the bathtub or write a poem. Sonny was going to baby-sit the twins so that his mom could have a rest.

"She won't rest with you baby-sitting," said Roger.

Sonny hit Roger on the arm and Roger tripped him and Mrs. Peters glared at them both.

"I'm giving my mom lightbulbs," said Tim. "Ones that are burned out."

Everyone stared at Tim.

"I might put some in the Easter basket too," he said.

"Why?" demanded Kevin.

"So she can paint them, what do you think?" said Tim. "You paint them and use them for Christmas tree ornaments."

"How did Christmas get into this?" whispered Lisa.

But Mrs. Peters said, "Good, Tim," and then Molly remembered that Tim collected old lightbulbs. When the Pee Wees had re-cycled, he had told them about painting them for ornaments.

Everyone seemed to have some plan but Molly. Even Mary Beth said she was go-ing to set her mom's hair the night before, and that was surely something original, Molly thought.

"I can't think of anything special," said Molly.

"You will," said Mary Beth.

"You can come to The Trout Farm with us," said Rachel kindly.

That was nice of Rachel, but Molly didn't feel like catching a fish in a tank.

"I'll help you think of something," said Rachel.

The Pee Wees ate the cupcakes Mrs. Stone had brought in (Sonny's mother was assistant troop leader), and then Mrs. Peters said, "Let's talk about the Easter baskets now, so that we all have something in mind for our badges, and so that we'll be able to brighten the seniors' holiday at the nursing home."

Everyone talked about the baskets, and what he or she would put in them besides the eggs. Then Mrs. Stone brought in the hard-boiled eggs to dye. She showed them how to write a message like "Happy Easter" on them with a crayon. After they were dyed, the writing showed up on the egg in white.

"This is fun!" said Tracy, who had a big blob of blue dye on the front of her blouse.

Sonny was trying to dye Roger's hair green when his mother caught him and took him to the laundry room for a talk.

Rachel had brought some dye that turned an egg many colors, and she showed Molly how to make one look just like marble. It was the prettiest one in Molly's basket. She wondered if she could take it out and give it to her mother for Mother's Day, but then she remembered the people in the nursing home who might need to be cheered up more than her mother. Anyway, the eggs probably wouldn't keep that long.

When everyone was finished and the baskets were complete, Mrs. Peters put

them in the middle of the table to be admired.

"Now, on Saturday you bring the other things to go in the basket, and I'll put some candy in each one, and we will deliver them," she said. "Be here at noon sharp."

They sang their Pee Wee song and left for home, most of them covered in as much dye as the Easter eggs.

On the way home Rachel said, "I'm going to put lots of little things in my basket that my senior would like, like needles and thread, and some paper clips and a manicure scissors and a nail file. Stuff she might run out of."

"I'm going to bring some of the little rabbit cookies my mom makes, with jelly beans for eyes," said Mary Beth.

"Those are good ideas," said Molly. "A lot better than old lightbulbs."

The three girls laughed, thinking about Tim's basket.

"He's poor," said Rachel.

"Well, it's a very creative thing to do," said Mary Beth.

When Molly got home her parents were talking in the den. They didn't hear her come in. Their voices were muffled, but Molly thought she heard her mom say "And what I'd really like, more than anything . . ."

Molly walked down the hall to listen. This might be a clue to what her mother wanted for Mother's Day! Something that could be a big surprise! Something to help Molly get that badge!

Molly could hardly make out the words her parents were saying. Something sounded like "Zippers! Lots of them. I can't seem to find them when I need them."

Molly stretched her neck to hear better. She heard what she thought was "hurry" or maybe "worry." Or was it "jury"?

Molly got her notebook out of her backpack and wrote all of it down. Zippers were a funny thing to want. Especially a lot of them. In a hurry. But if that was what her mother wanted, Molly would see to it that she got her wish.

CHAPTER 6
Zipping Along

It was lucky that Molly had come home in time to overhear her parents' conversation! If she had been a little later she would have missed it. But now she came to the next problem: Where could she find zippers? Especially a lot of them? And in a hurry?

Maybe the word was not *hurry*. Maybe it was *worry* or *jury*! She'd have to cover all the bases. *Jury* did not seem to make any sense, so she discarded that thought.

But if zippers were a worry to her mother, it was very important she get them. And Molly could easily hurry, although she couldn't give her mom her gift before Mother's Day. That would be like opening Christmas presents early. It would ruin the holiday.

Molly got out the phone book and looked in the yellow pages under Z. Not a single zipper was listed. She knew that zippers were *in* things, like jeans and purses and jackets. But if her mother had wanted things *with* zippers, she would not have said "zippers." She would have said "purse" or "jeans" or "jackets." No, this much was very clear—she wanted just plain zippers.

Molly went upstairs and found an old sweater of hers with holes in the elbows. Some of the yarn was unraveling. It was worn out and it was too small. Molly could take out the zipper and have her first gift!

She got a scissors and tried to cut out the zipper. But then it looked ragged and uneven. She decided she'd have to rip out the tiny stitches one by one. She sighed. It was a slow job. It would take forever.

"I hope all of them don't take this long," she said to herself. But she shouldn't complain. All the work would be worth it when her mother opened the gift! She would be surprised that Molly had known exactly what she wanted! Molly could just see the joy on her mother's face when she opened it!

No, the work would be worth it. She smoothed the zipper out flat. It isn't very nice-looking, as zippers go, she thought. And when she got it halfway up (or

down), it stuck. Well, there would be other zippers. All she had to do was find them.

The next day at school Molly was in a good mood. Knowing what to do for her mother, and for the badge, was half the battle. She had a good start. Now if only she could think of what to get for the Easter basket, she'd feel even better.

When the bell rang she walked home with Rachel and Ashley because Mary Beth was at the dentist.

"Have you decided what to do for Mother's Day?" asked Rachel.

Molly couldn't wait to tell them.

"I'm getting my mom zippers!" she said. "It's a lot of trouble, but it will be worth it. I heard her tell my dad it's what she wants."

The girls stopped walking.

"Zippers like in this backpack?" said Rachel.

Molly nodded.

"Does your mom sew?" asked Ashley.

"Sometimes," said Molly.

"Well, that makes sense," said Ashley. "But it's really best to get zippers and thread and stuff when you start to make something because of the color of the material. You have to match it."

Molly hadn't thought about the color. "I'll get her lots of colors," she said. "Then no matter what color she needs, she'll have it."

That must be why her mother had said "lots." It all made sense now. How practical her mother was!

"Have you got any old clothes you're throwing out that have zippers?" asked Molly.

Rachel frowned. "I don't think you should give someone a used gift," she said.

"I know where you can get new ones real cheap," said Ashley. "I was in the Sew Sew shop with my mom Saturday in the new mall, and they have what they call seconds in these huge baskets, and they're only a nickel apiece."

A nickel! Molly had lots of nickels in her bank! Or she could take a dollar from her allowance and buy lots and lots of zippers for that amount! And the new mall was just at the top of the hill. It was within walking distance!

"They're all different colors too," said Ashley.

"Let's go now!" said Molly.

The girls agreed to go along and show Molly the zipper basket at the Sew Sew shop.

Molly raced home to get her money and tell her mother she was going to the mall with Rachel and Ashley.

When they got there Ashley ran ahead and found the baskets. "Five cents!" she said, holding up a purple zipper for Molly to see. "What a bargain!"

This was a dream come true. Molly went through the baskets carefully and chose a zipper in every color. She chose six short ones and four long ones. She chose five thick ones and five thin ones. She counted out twenty zippers, the number she could buy with one of her dollars. Her mother would never run out of zippers again in her whole life!

Molly looked at the zippers that were left behind. She hated to not buy them all. They were so colorful. And so cheap. All of a sudden she had a wonderful idea. It was as if one of Tim's lightbulbs had switched on in her mind! She went back to the basket and chose twenty more zippers.

Then she paid for them all and the girls started for home.

"That was very nice of you to help me get my badge," said Molly to her friends. "Thanks a lot," she added warmly.

"You're welcome," said Ashley. "Your mother will really be surprised."

On Saturday the Pee Wees met at Mrs. Peters's house to go to the nursing home. Everyone had brought things to put in the baskets with the eggs.

"What is that?" said Mary Beth, staring at Molly's basket. "What are those things in your Easter basket?"

"How pretty!" said Tracy. "You have the brightest basket of all."

Everyone was looking at Molly's basket. It was the most attractive one. Not only were the eggs bright, but there were blue and red and yellow and green and purple ribbonlike things sticking out of the grass.

"They're zippers!" said Molly. "I decided if my mom wanted zippers so bad, the people in the nursing home would like them too."

"Why, what a surprising thing to put in an Easter basket!" said Mrs. Peters. "Yours is the most imaginative Easter basket here, Molly."

"What do they do with zippers?" asked Sonny.

"They can put them in shirts and dresses and stuff when they sew," said Molly.

"Those old geezers can't sew," said Roger. "They have bad eyesight. Anyway, what if a guy gets it? Men don't sew."

"Men can sew as well as women, Roger," said Mrs. Peters. "And it is rude to call people names."

"Even if they can't sew," said Patty

Baker, "they can just look at them. They're like a giant bouquet."

Mrs. Peters packed the baskets into the van. Then the Pee Wees piled in. When they got to the nursing home, the children tumbled out of the van. Loaded down with baskets full of treats and eggs, they went through the front doorway.

An elderly man smiled. "Look," he cried, "here come eggs with legs!" The Pee Wees laughed. They realized their faces were hidden behind the tall baskets! They set the baskets down on a table nearby and introduced themselves to all the senior citizens.

The seniors made a big fuss over the holiday visit and the baskets. They all admired Molly's zippers. Even the nurses asked how she had thought of such a clever Easter decoration.

Then one of the men played the piano in the community room, and the whole group sang "Here Comes Peter Cottontail" and "Easter Parade." Some of the women modeled their Easter bonnets. Others got out pictures of past Easters with their families and their many grandchildren.

It felt good to Molly to cheer these people up. When you cheer someone else up, you start to feel good yourself, she thought.

And Patty was right, no matter what Roger said. Even if no one used the zippers, they were fun just to look at.

CHAPTER 7
Slippery Zippers

The next weekend the Pee Wees raked the park. Then they went to a number of homes where people needed help with their yardwork. Molly washed windows and scrubbed lawn furniture.

The others helped load leaves and trash into Mr. Peters's pickup truck. By the end of the day, they were tired and hungry.

"The Tuesday after Mother's Day," said their leader, "we will get out new badges. You have all worked very hard for this badge. You've really earned it."

It had been fun helping clean up the park, thought Molly.

It had been fun visiting the nursing home.

And it would be fun having Easter dinner at her grandma's house!

When she got home Easter evening, Molly crossed everything off the list in her notebook except "Mother's Day."

The days passed quickly, and Molly spent time looking for just the right box for her mother's gift. She looked in the attic and in the closets, but none of the boxes she found was right. She couldn't ask her parents to find her one. That would spoil the surprise.

When she told Mary Beth about her problem, her friend said, "My mom just got a big box of yogurt pretzels, and we can put them in something else and you can have the box. It has a plastic top and you can see through it!"

The girls ran to look, and Molly said, "It's pretty big for the zippers."

"You have to put tissue paper in first," said Mary Beth. "Then you spread out the zippers on top, and when your mom unwraps it, she'll see all the pretty colors!"

Molly had to agree it would make a nice impression. The girls put the pretzels in a plastic bag and sealed it. Then they washed out the pretzel box and dried it. They dashed back to Molly's and filled it with pink tissue paper and the zippers.

"It's gorgeous!" said Mary Beth. "No other mother will get anything like it!"

Mary Beth was right, Molly was sure of that. But would Molly's mom like her gift better than catching her own fish at The Trout Farm? Molly hoped so.

After Mary Beth left, Molly wrapped the big round box in flowered paper. It wasn't easy to wrap a round box, and it was a little lumpy. She put a big yellow bow over the biggest lump to hide it.

The next morning Molly heard her dad up early getting breakfast. Before long he brought a tray to Molly's mom in bed, and a tray for Molly too.

Molly followed him into her parents' bedroom. "I'm not a mother!" she giggled.

"No, but I wouldn't be a father if it wasn't for you!" he said.

After they ate their French toast and scrambled eggs, Molly took out her box.

"Happy Mother's Day," she said. "I think it's just what you wanted."

"Why, what a pretty, big box!" said her dad.

Mrs. Duff tore off the wrapping, saying, "I can't imagine what it can be!"

Molly couldn't imagine how her mother *couldn't* imagine what it was! After all, she had said it out loud! When the wrapping was off, Molly waited for her mother to shout "Just what I wanted! Zippers! And I wanted them in a hurry!"

But she didn't. She just stared at the colorful zippers in their little plastic house, on their bed of tissue paper. She had a quizzical look on her face. Mr. Duff stared too.

"What is this pretty thing?" asked her mother finally.

"It's what you asked for!" said Molly. "Zippers!"

"Why, thank you," said her mother. "What a . . . nice gift. But I don't remember asking for zippers."

"I heard you!" said Molly. Things were not going as she'd planned. Just as with Roger's April Fool, *she* was the one who was surprised! Why were her holiday surprises always backfiring?

"You were upstairs in the den, and I heard you tell Dad that what you wanted real bad were zippers. Lots of zippers, because you never could find them."

A smile spread slowly over Mrs. Duff's face. At the same time Mr. Duff began to laugh out loud.

Mrs. Duff came and gave Molly a big hug. "How thoughtful," she said, "to get me what I wanted! But I think what I said was 'slippers,' not 'zippers'. 'Furry slippers.' I never can find my slippers when I want to put them on."

Molly felt like a fool. How silly this box of zippers must look to her parents! It was April Fools' Day all over again. Her parents would tell this funny story to their friends, just as Roger had! She would be the laughingstock of the town!

"I like these zippers better," said her mother. "Really I do. I never have a zipper when I need one, and I never think to buy them!"

"Anyway," said Mr. Duff, taking a big box from behind his back, "it wouldn't be a good idea for both of us to give your mom the same thing!"

And there inside Mr. Duff's box were furry slippers for Mrs. Duff! Two pairs, one blue and one pink!

"All's well that ends well," said Molly's mom. "I love both gifts very much."

On Tuesday at the Pee Wee meeting, everyone told about giving her or his gift.

"My dad liked his steak!" said Roger.

"My mom liked her fish too," said Rachel. "It wasn't as easy to catch as you'd think." She glared at Roger.

"How did your mother like her zippers?" Mrs. Peters asked Molly. "Was she surprised?"

"Yes, she was," said Molly. "And she liked them a lot. It was just what she wanted." There was no need to confess the misunderstanding when it had all ended so well.

Then, one by one, Mrs. Peters called out names for badges. Everyone got one. The badge had a little green tree—for spring, their leader told them. And under the tree was an egg, brightly colored.

Molly ran her fingers over the smooth, silky stitching on the tree. Nothing in the world felt as good as a fresh, new badge! And this one felt twice as good because she had worked so hard for it!

As they joined hands and sang the Pee

Wee song, Molly was very, very glad to have her friends around her to share in the Pee Wee warmth and fun.

Rat's knees, it was great to be a Pee Wee!

Even with Roger in the troop.

Pee Wee Scout Song

(to the tune of
"Old MacDonald Had a Farm")

Scouts are helpers, Scouts have fun,
Pee Wee, Pee Wee Scouts!
We sing and play when work is done,
Pee Wee, Pee Wee Scouts!

With a good deed here,
And an errand there,
Here a hand, there a hand,
Everywhere a good hand.

Scouts are helpers, Scouts have fun,
Pee Wee, Pee Wee Scouts!

 **Pee Wee Scout Pledge**

We love our country
And our home,
Our school and neighbors too.

As Pee Wee Scouts
We pledge our best
In everything we do.

'Even if ... can't sew,' said Patty